ESCAPE FROM THE POP-UP PRISON

BY MICHAEL DAHL
ILLUSTRATED BY BRADFORD KENDALL

Librarian Reviewer
Laurie K. Holland
Media Specialist (National Board Certified), Edina, MN
MA in Elementary Education, Minnesota State University, Mankato

Reading Consultant
Elizabeth Stedem
Educator/Consultant, Colorado Springs, CO
MA in Elementary Education, University of Denver, CO

STONE ARCH BOOKS
Minneapolis   San Diego

Zone Books are published by Stone Arch Books
151 Good Counsel Drive, P.O. Box 669
Mankato, Minnesota 56002
www.stonearchbooks.com

Library of Congress Cataloging-in-Publication Data
Dahl, Michael.
    Escape from the Pop-up Prison / by Michael Dahl; illustrated
by Bradford Kendall.
    p. cm. — (Zone Books — Library of Doom)
    ISBN 978-1-4342-0490-5 (library binding)
    ISBN 978-1-4342-0550-6 (paperback)
    [1. Books and reading—Fiction. 2. Librarians—Fiction.
3. Fantasy.] I. Kendall, Bradford, ill. II. Title.
PZ7.D15134Esc 2008
[Fic]—dc22
2007032223

Summary: A girl follows a group of strangers inside the giant
Library of Doom. The strangers want their evil friends released
from the pages a pop-up book. Can the Librarian stop them before
the world's deadliest criminals are set free?

Creative Director: Heather Kindseth
Senior Designer for Cover and Interior: Kay Fraser
Graphic Designer: Brann Garvey

1 2 3 4 5 6 13 12 11 10 09 08

Printed in the United States of America

TABLE OF CONTENTS

The Library of Doom is the world's largest collection of strange and dangerous books. The Librarian's duty is to keep the books from falling into the hands of those who would use them for evil purposes.

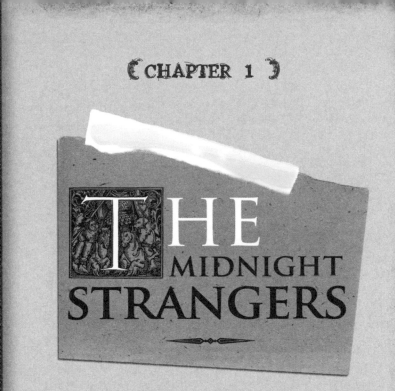

CHAPTER 1

THE MIDNIGHT STRANGERS

A girl **wakes** up at midnight.

She hears strange voices coming from <u>downstairs.</u>

She **creeps** out of her room to see who it is.

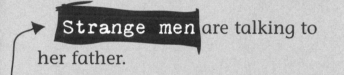

Strange men are talking to her father.

"You know the only way inside the Library," one of the men says. "Take us there, or else."

Who are they? the girl wonders.

The men **force** her father out of the house.

From a safe distance, the girl **follows** them.

She hides in the **shadows**.

The men walk through dozens of **dark streets** and **alleys**.

CHAPTER 2

THE WAY IN

In a rundown part of town, the men stop in a small alley.

The girl's father points to an old poster on the wall. "That is the way in," he says.

"Show us," says one of
the men.

The girl's father pushes against one
of the letters.

A secret passageway appears.

"Follow me," the girl's father says.

The men all slip through the entrance.

Now the girl knows where her father is taking the men.

They are **entering** a secret
hallway that leads to the
Library of Doom.

{ CHAPTER 3 }

THE PAPER TRAIL

The girl's father had once worked in the Library of Doom.

He had been a **page,** an assistant to the mysterious Librarian.

The girl knows that the Librarian and her father had been good friends.

Now, as the girl follows the
men, she sees the passage end at a
huge pit.

"We need to get to the other side!"
exclaims one of the men. "There is no
way across. Is this a **trick**?"

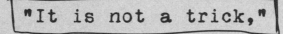

"It is not a trick," says the girl's father.

He pulls a book from the inside of his jacket.

Then he **throws** the book into the pit.

The book flies open. Its pages
scatter through the air.

Then the pages form themselves
into a long bridge.

"This is the only way across,"
says the girl's father.

CHAPTER 4

THE POP-UP PRISON

On the other side of the vast pit is a huge, **stone platform.**

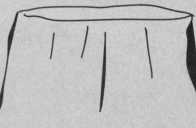

In the middle of the platform sits a single book.

"There it is!" shouts one of the men. "That's what we've come for."

The strangers **open** the book.

As they turn a page, a `prison cell` pops up out of the book.

There is a man trapped inside the cell.

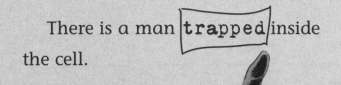

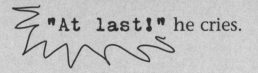

"At last!" he cries.

The strangers free the man.

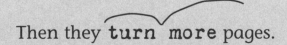

Then they turn more pages.

On each page, another cell pops up with another prisoner inside.

The strangers **release** each prisoner.

The girl watches fearfully from the shadows.

"It is the Pop-up Prison," she says to herself. "The world's **deadliest criminals** were trapped in its pages."

What will happen now that they are **free?**

CHAPTER 5

FREE!

A bright light **flashes** from the huge pit.

It is the Librarian.

"What have you done?" he cries.

One of the strangers **shakes** his
fist at the Librarian.

"Too late, Librarian," he shouts.
"We have freed our friends."

"You will never be able to defeat
all of us," the other man yells. "We
are **too strong** for you."

The girl **runs** to her father.

"How could you do this?" she asks. "Why did you **betray** the Librarian?"

"Your father warned me," the Librarian tells her. "As soon as he pressed that poster, a `signal` told me he was here."

"So what?" says one of the prisoners. "We are free. Now we can `rule the world!`"

The Librarian smiles.

"You are not in the world. You are in the `Library of Doom`," he says. "And here, I rule."

The father pulls his daughter to the paper bridge.

As they run across the bridge, the pages **fall away** behind them.

The criminals **yell** and **scream** from the stone platform.

"Don't worry," the father tells the girl. "As I said, this was the only way in."

"And your father **never lies,**" says the Librarian.

Then the Librarian adds, "My pages can always be trusted."

∽ THE END ∾

A PAGE FROM THE LIBRARY OF DOOM

MORE ABOUT POP-UP AND MOVABLE BOOKS

Pop-up books have been around for hundreds of years. They were originally known as "movable books" since objects and sections in them moved.

The first movable books were printed for adults, not children. One of the earliest movables, printed in Switzerland in 1543, was a book on anatomy. It showed the inside of a human body in different layers.

Dean & Son, a publisher in Great Britain in the 1800s, made the first pop-up books designed specifically for children. The books contained a special ribbon with each page. When the ribbon was pulled, the page would open up into a 3-dimensional display.

The person who designs the pop-ups for a book is called a **paper engineer**.

Today's pop-up books are all made by hand. Most of them are assembled in Central America or Singapore.

It may take as many as 60 people to put together one pop-up book.

Modern pop-up books have been made that contain electric lights and recorded music.

Robert Sabuda and Matthew Reinhart are wizards of modern pop-up books. They are famous for their pop-ups on prehistoric creatures. Some of their books use more than one hundred pieces of paper to help create the 3-D effects.

ABOUT THE AUTHOR

Michael Dahl is the author of more than 100 books for children and young adults. He has twice won the AEP Distinguished Achievement Award for his nonfiction. His Finnegan Zwake mystery series was chosen by the Agatha Awards to be among the five best mystery books for children in 2002 and 2003. He collects books on poison and graveyards, and lives in a haunted house in Minneapolis, Minnesota.

ABOUT THE ILLUSTRATOR

Bradford Kendall has enjoyed drawing for as long as he can remember. As a boy, he loved to read comic books and watch old monster movies. He graduated from the Rhode Island School of Design with a BFA in Illustration. He has owned his own commercial art business since 1983, and lives in Providence, Rhode Island, with his wife, Leigh, and their two children Lily and Stephen. They also have a cat named Hansel and a dog named Gretel.

GLOSSARY

assistant (uh-SIS-tuhnt)—a person who helps somebody else

betray (bi-TRAY)—to reveal a secret and break someone's trust

mysterious (miss-TIHR-ee-uhs)—hard to explain or understand

page (PAYJ)—a young servant or assistant

passageway (PASS-ij-way)—a secret tunnel that people use to pass from one place to another

platform (PLAT-form)—a flat surface that is high off the ground

rundown (RUHN-doun)—old and needing repairs

signal (SIG-nuhl)—something done to communicate a warning, such as a noise or movement

vast (VAST)—very large in size

DISCUSSION QUESTIONS

1. Do you think it was safe for the girl to follow her father and the strange men? What would you have done?

2. The girl's father was forced to reveal the secret location of the Library of Doom. Is it okay to share some secrets with others? Why or why not?

3. If you could be trapped inside of a book, what book would you choose? Explain your answer.

WRITING PROMPTS

1. In this book, the author didn't reveal too much information about the girl. That's part of what makes the story mysterious. Use your imagination and write more about this character.

2. Pretend you are one of the criminals trapped on the stone platform. Describe how you would escape from the Library of Doom.

3. Family members make great characters for a book. Write about one or more of your family members.

INTERNET SITES

The book may be over, but the adventure is just beginning.

Do you want to read more about the subjects or ideas in this book? Want to play cool games or watch videos about the authors who write these books? Then go to FactHound. At *www.facthound.com*, you'll be able to do all that, and more. The FactHound website can also send you to other safe Internet sites.

Check it out!